Quest *of the* Bloodline

The Trial (Book 1)

Quest of the Bloodline
The Trial (Book 1)
Copyright © 2018 by Rose Ethridge

All rights reserved. No part of this publication may be reproduced, distributed, or transmitted in any form or by any means, including photocopying, recording, or other electronic or mechanical methods, without the prior written permission of the publisher or author, except in the case of brief quotations embodied in critical reviews and certain other noncommercial uses permitted by copyright law.

Although every precaution has been taken to verify the accuracy of the information contained herein, the author and publisher assume no responsibility for any errors or omissions. No liability is assumed for damages that may result from the use of information contained within.

Library of Congress Control Number: 2018954687
ISBN-13:   Paperback: 978-1-950073-00-9
                  e-book: 978-1-950073-02-3

Printed in the United States of America

GoToPublish
1-800-539-0988
www.gotopublish.com
info@gotopublish.com

Quest *of the* Bloodline

The Trial (Book 1)

Rose Ethridge

Contents

Chapter One 1
Chapter Two 9
Chapter Three 19
Chapter Four 29
Chapter Five 37
Chapter Six 45
Chapter Seven 53
Chapter Eight 65

Chapter One

I jerked my fingers through my tangled hair, trying to tame it into something dignified and airy. Not an easy task given the thickness and the brazen red color. Add on to that a late evening, and it would be a miracle if it looked anything close to normal.

"Heldens is going to kill me," I muttered to myself as I raced up the stairs toward the early night classrooms. Heldens was my history teacher, and she had a delightful dislike for me that could only be categorized under disdain. I should have been grateful it wasn't pure, unadulterated hatred, but it was hard when my grades were suffering for it. I could not get another C in history.

And, okay, I didn't help myself out any by periodically being late to aforementioned class. But how could anyone blame me? I was a late sleeper and history was already so hard to focus on.

I shot my hand out to catch the pole of the railing and swung myself around the corner as I reached the top of the stairs. And then promptly threw myself into a very hard wall that felt suspiciously like a chest. The impact sent me spiraling backward, landing badly on my butt and nearly stumbling back down the stairs I'd just run up.

But a large, strong hand shot out and caught my shoulders before that happened.

When I finally forced myself to see who I'd just embarrassed myself in front of, I was horrified to see that it was none other than Alexandre Petrovic. Otherwise known as the hottest vampire in Holloway Boarding. His silky, dark hair had fallen forward, even darker against his smooth, pale skin. It wasn't quite long enough to get into his eyes, but it was close. By the time my eyes got to his mouth, he was grinning.

I winced. "Uh, sorry."

He laughed at me; the sound had an almost musical, lulling quality. He is the kind of vampire people expects when they think *Prince of Darkness*—which only made sense, he *is* a Petrovic. Despite his laughter, he still helped me up, reminding me that he still had his hands wrapped around my arms.

"What's your hurry?" he asked with that same musical quality in his tone.

Brushing off the pleats of my skirt, I cleared my throat and tried to regain some dignity. "I, uh, I'm running a little late." As soon as I said it, I noticed that *he* had to be running late too. We had history together. Frowning, I was about to point this out when he cut me off.

"Well, if that's all it is, maybe we should just ditch. Together. Since we're both already going to be late." He winked at me, leaning forward as he spoke as though whispering some great secret into my ear.

For a second, I gaped at him. Ditch? Together? There was a glorious moment where I truly considered that opportunity to spend that kind of alone time with him—would we go to the fountain? Maybe wander the thick woods surrounding the Klatch? Or maybe just find a clearing where we could…

I jolted myself back to reality as I dismissed the thoughts and reminded myself that even if the time somehow went like that, I would still have to come back and face the wrath of Heldens. That was like a bucket of cold water.

Shaking my head, I began to walk toward class as I answered, "Ditching might be okay for a Petrovic, but for me that's like begging for another month of detention."

He laughed again, easily keeping step beside me. "Well, then at least let me walk you."

Technically, he already *was* walking me, but the fact that he brought it up was enough to make my heart try to kick out an extra beat. My pale cheeks even worked overtime to blush. I glanced up at him through my lashes, trying to be discreet, but he caught me. His grin widened.

I wasn't an idiot. I knew how social stratification worked, and I knew that I did not rank high on anyone's list of Attractive Vampires—or *liked* vampires. I was the ugly duckling, as a matter of fact, and no one was going to tell me otherwise. While Alexandre, however, was on the complete opposite end of the scale. His hotness reigned supreme at Holloway Boarding.

So why was he offering to walk me to class?

Before I could figure out what I was supposed to say—okay, I was supposed to say *no*, but I really didn't want to—he nudged me a little with his shoulder. "C'mon. It'll be easier if you walk in with a Petrovic, right?"

And how was I supposed to argue with that?

Offering a small smile, I nodded. "Um, yeah. Alright. Sure."

The walk was awkward and I almost wished I'd just told him to leave me alone. Except that when I glanced over at him again, he was still grinning and didn't seem to mind the heavy silence hanging between us, or the fact that he was walking with *me*. To anyone else, that would be social suicide.

Of course, as a Petrovic, he was the epitome of cool, and I guessed that meant he could make up his own rules.

We stopped outside the door to class and, once again, awkwardness pressed in against us. Or at least, it did me. *He* seemed perfectly calm and collected, like we walked together every evening to class after I fell on my butt.

I wasn't quite sure what the next move was—do we go in together? Should I say thanks and count my lucky stars that I was graced with his presence?

Before I could figure it out, Alexandre turned to me and smiled. "Ready for the wrath of Heldens?" he asked, winking as he did so.

I gave a nervous laugh, trying to tone down my obviously over-reddened cheeks. "Um, not really."

He considered me for a long moment, then leaned in close so he could whisper to me. "It's not too late. We could still take off. Disappear for the day. No one would even miss us."

His eyes were deep pools of chipped ice, beckoning me like sirens to give in to his whims and desires. It wasn't quite a thrall—a vampire couldn't thrall another vampire—but it was close. It was a power possessed only by the oldest families. My dad may have belonged somewhere in the vicinity of the Petrovics as far as that list was concerned, but my mother's common blood had tainted me. It was what everyone had told me since my birth.

And it was the reason that I dropped his gaze, pulling away before I said something stupid like *yes*. Clearing my throat, I shook my head. "I really can't afford that much detention. My birthday's coming up, you know?"

I peeked up at him to see a disappointed look on his face. It piqued my curiosity, but before I could ask him what that was all about, he offered me a rueful smile and pushed open the door to hold it open for me. "Another time then."

I managed a dumbfounded nod, then strode into the classroom. It was quiet like the grave. As close to literally as you can get.

As soon as I took one footstep inside, every eye in the place was staring at me. A sea of cool vampire-blue eyes stared back at me, unblinking, and as close to ice as you could get. Even the professor's eyes were the same, eternally youthful and even soulless. It sent chills down my spine, but that might have just been because I knew I was on Heldens's naughty list.

Behind me, Alexandre cleared his throat. I felt his cool hand against my lower back, urging me forward into the classroom. I shivered at the touch, but tried to ignore it. My first stumbling steps told me I wasn't successful.

"Apologies, Ms. Heldens. I'm afraid I've made Miss Nightshade very late. You'll have to forgive her."

Ms. Heldens looked like she wanted to do anything but forgive me, but even she had difficulties arguing with a Petrovic. In the classroom, she was technically in charge, but in the Klatch, that was all the Petrovic line. Alexandre may have had several older brothers who might take charge after their father, but Alexandre always seemed to have the most sway. More powerful, more in control.

Eventually, Ms. Heldens pursed her lips and sent me a scathing glare, but ultimately dismissed us both to our seats.

Although I was intensely grateful for the reprieve from yet more punishment, I couldn't help but be a little irritated with her reaction. *It must be nice to come from a family of power*, I reflected as I headed toward the very back of the class where I always sat. *Or any family at all.*

Alexandre headed toward his saved seat next to Dahlia, the prettiest vampire in the school—and his Promised. They were set to marry by twenty-one, which meant they were technically off limits to anyone else.

Not that that seemed to stop them. Alexandre liked to flirt whenever the mood suited him and Dahlia had slept with half the guys at school. Hardly what I'd consider a devoted, loving marriage, but it was arranged so it would last.

Part of me thought they were lucky. Two beautiful vampires already paired up, their futures filled with promise. The rest of me thought it was kind of sad, because sometimes I got the feeling that they didn't even like each other.

I let my gaze trace over Alexandre's beautiful profile. He looked bored, like some ancient Romanian painting depicting the young prince stuck in the meetings that would teach him to rule.

I almost laughed at the thought because it wasn't that far from the truth.

My eyes lingered on the power couple for several seconds longer. When I sensed Alexandre turning to glance toward me, probably feeling my intense stare, I jerked my eyes away and stared at my desk. There were several hundred years' worth of doodled designs covering it in varying shades of faded. I'd contributed several of them, but my art hardly compared to the gruesome depictions of vampiric death. Bodies burst into flames from sunlight. Blood poured from their opened veins. Hunters pounded silver stakes through the hearts of beautiful, but tragic vampires. And the beheading...

The images sent shivers through me just as they always did.

There are many ways to die as a human, but only a few will work against a vampire. And they are some of the worst ways to go, in my humble opinion. It's the reason why we're so secluded, here in the Carpathian wilderness, hidden in the mountains like relics from a time forgotten. The world tries to forget about us and move on, but this area seems immune to time. For better or worse.

It's been a hundred years since anyone's seen a human around here—and that was for the best. For our sake and theirs.

At the front of the class, Heldens was droning on about just that. "Obviously, our interactions with humans have been limited. It is by their own idiotic prejudices that we were forced to isolate ourselves from them. The Klatch settled here years ago, putting up the wards that misdirect the humans." She wrote a name across the chalkboard, the chalk screeching as though in pain. I winced.

Did she really have to write that? I thought in irritation. *Is there a person in the class that doesn't know it?*

"Van Helsing," she read, underlining it for emphasis. "They are the most dangerous of humans. Known simply as Hunters, they have sought out our kind for centuries. They have killed us mercilessly, believing themselves to be on some holy mission from God." She smiled wryly and several students snickered.

I rolled my eyes. I didn't know about holy missions or anything, but I knew it had been a long time since there had been a Van Helsing around here. Long enough that I was willing to bet they had all died out.

Thank god.

Every gruesome picture scribbled on my desk represented what the Van Helsings did to my kind. Better they're all dead.

Heldens spent the rest of the period droning on about the Van Helsings, the history of humanity's violent offenses toward our kind, and every other boring thing she could think of. I tried to focus, but mostly ended up adding more doodles to the table in front of me until I ran out of space.

Chapter Two

When class let out, I was relieved. History was by far my worst subject and my wandering mind hardly helped me out. Students hurried to the door and I followed suit, willing myself to get out of there as quickly as possible before any other craziness could happen this morning. Or worse, Heldens changed her mind about giving me detention. Yet even as I made it to the door, I couldn't help but glance back at Alexandre and Dahlia. They've lingered while everyone else passed, and maybe it was just me, but it looked like they were arguing. When Alexandre glanced up from Dahlia to catch my gaze, I quickly twisted away and hurried out the door.

Jeez, he probably thought I was a freak.

Once in the hallway, I received the snubbed treatment that was typical of my day. Pretty much every vamp in the school made a point of ignoring me—except Corrine. Although ninety percent of vamps were picture-perfect, every once in a while, you got one that was a little odd. Not tall enough or skinny enough or pale enough. Corrine was the first two, and I was the last. It was the main reason we'd become friends in the first place.

Her curvy, little body came barreling out of another classroom and straight for me. She slammed into me a second later. I gasped out, "Corrine!"

Pulling away, she slipped her arm into mine and began steering me toward the stairs. Tossing her head of jet-black hair, she cocked her head and gave me a sly glance. "So, rumor has it—"

"It's six at night! There can't be a rumor yet!" I protested, my voice taking on a whiney quality to it.

She ignored me. "Rumor has it that you were spotted walking with Mr. King Hottie himself."

I refused to look at her because I knew that my expression was a mixture of embarrassed and panicked. I considered trying to steer the subject away from Alexandre and our early evening run-in, but I doubted I would have a snowball's chance in the Underworld at deterring her from the subject. Like basically every other female vamp in the place, she was kind of obsessed with him.

"Bronwyn!" she exclaimed when I didn't answer. "Oh my Hades, it's totally true!"

I let my head hang and my shoulders slump as I mumbled a defeated, "What are they saying?"

Corrine let out a loud squealing sound full of excitement. She then launched into a long list of who had said what. I had just a moment to wonder how on earth so many people had heard about this when it had only happened about an hour ago. "...and Cynthia said that you two were doing it in the closet by the—"

I stopped her dead in her tracks and forced her to swivel around and face me. My face was burning hot, but it was in indignation more than anything else. "I did *not* do anything with him in the closet!"

Corrine laughed a little, waving off my outrage. "Obviously. I mean, have you even kissed a guy?"

Narrowing my eyes at her, I folded my arms across my chest and we began walking again. Grudgingly, I said, "No."

"I knew most of it was just gossip, Brownie," she told me in as soothing a voice as possible. She even used my childhood nickname—which I'd never decided if I liked or not—as she patted my shoulder. "Honestly, I figured it was just a normal glance from across the hallway that got blown way out of proportion. I had no idea you actually spent time with him!"

"I didn't spend time with him," I argued. "It was more, like, walking in awkward silence."

"Which means you guys walked to class together!"

I let out a long-suffering sigh, even as my stomach knotted itself up and tried to strangle the butterflies growing there. It was nothing. Absolutely nothing. He just wanted someone to ditch with. "Can we *please* talk about something else?"

She rolled her pretty blue eyes at me. "What could possibly be more important than the biggest gossip right now?"

I was silent for a long moment as it occurred to me that there *was* something more important than my Alexandre gossip. And it probably was the reason that Corrine was obsessing so much about this. Chewing on my lower lip, I thought about it. Corrine was finally seventeen. We'd had her big birthday party last weekend, complete with an all-day party filled with creepy stories, lots of blood velvet cake, and dressing up like glam queens. It had only been the two of us because Corrine was almost as unpopular as I was, but it had been fun.

Now that party seemed like ages ago, and I couldn't deny the welling pit of dread in my gut. Tonight, she went to the Klatch.

"How are you doing?" I finally asked in a small voice.

I saw Corrine's features blanch, but her bright smile came back a second later. "What are you talking about? I'm excellent!"

"Corrine, seriously. I know that I would be terrified to meet the Klatch." Actually, I *was* terrified. My own meeting was steadily approaching and it had me on edge. It was how I knew that Corrine had to be putting on a brave face.

After a moment, I saw that brave face slip. "I am. I totally am. What if I completely fail? What if they—"

"They're not going to exile you," I quickly interrupted. "No one's been exiled in generations."

She didn't look entirely convinced, which I thought was a little weird. Sure, exile was always brought up whenever a new vamp came of age, but it was always just a passing threat. The kind that parents used to keep their kids in line.

Not that I'd know; mine had been dead since I was only a year old.

"You're right," Corrine said. But she didn't look any more at ease.

Bumping my shoulder into hers, I gave her a smile. "C'mon, it's just a stupid task. It's probably something ridiculous, like picking flowers from the woods or finding the first leaf of fall. They just try to make it all intimidating so that we'll be scared."

Corrine let out a laugh. It was still nervous, still shaky, but at least it sounded somewhat relieved. "You're right. I'm just letting them get in my head."

We both laughed and the farther we walked, the better we both felt. I couldn't tell her what her trial would be; no one could. Trials were forever private. No one was allowed to talk about them, not now or in a hundred years. Corrine and I always joked that it was because the trials were really lame, but the Klatch wanted to make everyone terrified to keep them in line. Then, everyone was just so embarrassed that they refused to speak of it afterward.

I wanted to believe that, but I understood why Corrine was scared. The closer I got to my own trial, the more nervous I became. Because even though we joked and laughed about it, there was always this kernel of doubt in the back of my mind.

What if the trials *were* something terrible? And what if I did fail?

❧

Corrine and I had two more classes together, one apart, then dinner. We sat together then, enjoying the cool evenings outside while we could. Fall would start to get too cold to enjoy, especially since we couldn't exactly go out in the sun to warm up. After dinner, I had my last class of the day, which was the equivalent length of two classes. Physical Education. Not my favorite, but we'd all been doing it for so long that even I couldn't be completely awful at it.

When class let out, I headed toward my dorm room. It was beneath the actual school on the bottom level with everyone else's for safety reasons. I was hoping to catch Corrine before sunrise, maybe at breakfast, since I knew she was so nervous about her trial.

I was so lost in thoughts of Corrine and her trial—and, okay, my trial too—that I didn't notice the group of girls following me down the stairs. There were three of them and most of the students were heading toward the dorms, so I didn't think anything of them.

Not until they stopped me.

One of the girls, Cynthia, shoved past me only to turn around abruptly right in front of me. She was the perfect vamp from her pale skin to her blue eyes. She tossed her glossy, black hair over one pale shoulder. Her mouth split into a wide grin, her long canines poking into her full lower lip.

I stopped before I ran into her and instinctively tried to back up, but her two friends—carbon copies of her—were there to stop me.

"What's your hurry?" asked the one over my left shoulder.

"Yeah. We just want to chat," continued the one over my right.

Pursing my lips together to keep from sighing in exasperation and defeat, I said nothing. Instead, I tried pushing past the girl in front in an effort to get into the common room. I hoped that maybe they'd be less bold in the company of others.

Cynthia caught me before I could get past her, her long fingers wrapping around my upper arm tightly. "I didn't say you could leave." Her voice was cool, menacing.

Not a good sign.

"I just wanted to get changed before breakfast," I mumbled, trying to wiggle free of her hold.

She held fast. "And what are you going to have for breakfast?" Her perfectly drawn eyebrows rose in question.

I glanced between her and the two girls behind me, then cleared my throat. "The same thing as everyone else."

Minion Number One on my left shoulder leaned closer to me and said, "Oh? Do they even offer virgin pudding?"

Blood pudding was traditionally offered every morning for breakfast, a quick way to get the sort of blood dose vamps needed to make it through the sleeping hours. Even if we didn't like the stuff—which, admittedly, I didn't really—we all had to eat it. Otherwise, we might wake up hungry and *that* was dangerous.

"Can I just get past, please?" I asked, realizing where they were going with this.

Minion Number Two leaned over my shoulder, setting her chin against my collarbone. She felt cold against my skin, another strike against my vampire heritage. "But seriously though. Are you even a vampire?" she quipped, grinning sharply at me.

I shrugged her off my shoulder and was able to break free of Cynthia's grasp. I tried to shove past her again, but once more, she blocked my path to the common room and theoretical safety. I looked her in those bright blue eyes, about to ask what she wanted from me, when I saw something in her hand. It was a glass, clear and filled with what was very clearly a thick, deep-red liquid. So red that it was practically black.

My mouth watered, even as a quick tendril of revulsion swept me. I didn't *like* blood, but I wanted it. It was instinct.

"Drink it," she said, offering it to me. When I hesitated, sure it was a trap, she pushed it a little closer. "Go on. Prove yourself."

Despite my churning stomach, I reached to accept the glass. It was a quick, easy way to prove that despite my unruly red hair and my easy-to-blush skin, I was still a vampire. I was still one of them. But as my fingers touched the slightly warm glass—Hades, it was fresh—Cynthia tilted the glass. She thrust it toward me and the contents emptied all over me.

The blood splattered across my outstretched hand, slipped down my neck and shirt, and some of it landed on my face. It smeared over my mouth and sprinkled my cheeks. I probably even got some in my hair, not that anyone would notice the red hiding there.

I stood frozen, staring at her with wide eyes.

I couldn't do anything. The three vamps started cackling, Cynthia moving so that she was standing beside me on the stairs. Leaning in, she said, "Good luck. The boys are hungry."

My eyes widened and I paled.

The three girls left me, heading up the stairs. I debated following them up, just to get away from what I knew awaited me below, but there was no point. They'd wait for me, make sure that I headed toward the dorms, not the classrooms upstairs.

Maybe they've already eaten, I tried to tell myself.

But it was pointless. No one had gone to breakfast yet. Which meant the boys were in their dorms, headed for the cafeteria, or... sitting in the common room.

I was practically shaking with the thought.

Boys weren't very good at controlling their bloodlust. They'd come at me. The blood would draw them like wolves to a fresh kill. And it wouldn't matter that I was one of them; they'd be hungry enough to bite me and try a bit before coming to their senses.

Assuming they did at all.

Fear shook me and I turned away from the commons. I had to get to the showers before anyone spotted me. On shaking legs, I started up the stairs, but I didn't get far. Coming down the stairs were two tall, attractive vampire boys. They were older than me, a year ahead, but that didn't matter. Boys had difficulties with cravings until their twenties, sometimes later.

And right now, they were definitely having difficulties.

I knew the second they smelled me. They froze simultaneously and their eyes went wide. The normally pale-blue color darkened until it was nothing but deep, hungry blackness. Their fangs elongated, protruding from their mouths into their lower lips.

"By Hades," I muttered, then swiveled around again.

I didn't even get a step because standing directly behind me was another boy. His eyes were already black with hunger, his teeth long and sharp. He was so close that I didn't even get the chance to jerk away before his hands wrapped around both of my upper arms. He jerked me toward him, and I braced myself for the pain that would come at any moment.

Oh, Hades, he's going to bite me.

But the bite never came.

"Get away from her!"

I was shocked by the sound of Alexandre's voice, my eyes jerking open in surprise. The vampire in front of me was ripped away with strength that was impressive even for a vamp. I stumbled back, nearly barreling into the two vampires behind me, but Alexandre—who had just finished throwing my attacker into the wall—grabbed me easily, and shoved me behind him. I stared at his back, wide-eyed and disbelieving as he growled at the other two vampires.

"Leave. *Now.*"

They thought it over for a half a second, then decided the meal wasn't worth it. The hunger was consuming, but self-preservation was still ingrained in them too. Especially since they weren't wild vampires. They'd been here their whole lives, just like me.

They turned in unison and ran back up the stairs where they'd come from. I glanced behind me to see that the vampire Alexandre had thrown was gone.

I was shaking, probably in shock, and while I should have been relieved, I couldn't help but notice that when I glanced back at Alexandre, his eyes were a deep black too. He had smelled the blood just as easily as they had, and now he was hungry.

I had just enough time to back myself up against the wall when he reached for me. I flinched as his fingers wrapped around my upper arm—how many times had I been grabbed there today? Too many, I decided.

I shook him off easily. There was no question that he'd let me. He didn't even look offended by it.

"I'll escort you to your room," he told me in a thick voice.

I almost opened my mouth to argue with him and inform him that I didn't need an escort, but thought better of it at the last minute. We still had to make it through the common room and if there were other vampires around, there was no guarantee that they'd be in as good control of their impulses as Alexandre seemed to be.

At least, I hope he is.

Nodding, I followed him the rest of the way down the stairs. I was surprised to see that the common room was empty and wondered if it had anything to do with Alexandre's presence or if it was just the terrified vampires running from him.

We said nothing as we walked, the atmosphere noticeably different from earlier that evening. But he never tried anything. Even as the blood lingered on my skin and clothes, he did nothing. I saw his nostrils flare a couple of times, and I knew that the hunger was still there by the dark of his eyes, but he didn't try anything.

I was impressed.

We stopped at my door and I turned so that my back was to it. "Um... thank you."

He clenched his jaw and closed his eyes, taking in a deep breath. He seemed to realize what a big mistake that was because a second later, he was about three feet farther from me. "You're welcome," he managed to get out. "But be more careful next time. Some vamps don't care what happens to a girl like you, Bronwyn."

He turned away then and stalked off, maybe to his own room or maybe to quench that fiery thirst that the smell of blood always evoked within us. When he was gone, I jerked open the door to my room and rushed in. I slumped to the floor and acknowledged two things.

First, I was miraculously alive, thanks to Alexandre. Which meant that he had a lot better control than I ever would have given him credit for and people really didn't care if I died. Which was scary.

Second, despite the blood that lingered on my skin and my clothes, I wasn't hungry. Even though my mouth watered and instinct dared me to lick at the blood near my lips, my stomach still churned at the thought.

I didn't know what that meant, and I certainly didn't know why it seemed that Alexandre Petrovic saved my butt twice in one night.

Chapter Three

I slept fitfully that day, tossing and turning. While I slept—or tried to—my mind was flooded with dreams. They weren't new, but they were just as disturbing as ever. Sometimes my dad was there, whispering awful things into my ear. Sometimes a beautiful woman lay in his arms, writhing, dying. But the worst one was the longest and it ended the worst. I was running through the woods toward the rising sun as people chased me. Humans. Fires burning from torches; cries echoing into the quickly approaching dawn.

Eventually, I'd reach the end of the woods. The trees would thin and open up into a clearing that went on forever. It stopped at the horizon and there I would see it. The sun. Lifting up slowly, slowly, each ray of light darting across the grassy clearing until they finally reached me.

They burned.

That was, thankfully, always when I woke up. When the dreams first started, I'd wake up screaming, but I'd grown used to them. Now I woke with a gasp, bolting up in my bed. Tears streamed down my face, and I clawed at my arms and exposed skin like it might still be burning.

Sunlight was a horrible death.

I trembled as I blinked in the darkness. Vampires could see in the dark, but it was like having cats' eyes or something. You could only see if there was some, any, light to reflect back. Right now, there wasn't even light slipping in from beneath the door. Complete blackout, which told me it was still daylight outside.

The thought made me shiver.

Stumbling around in the darkness, I shucked off my covers and fumbled for the lamp at my side. It was a gaslight because it was still more reliable than electricity—and probably saved everyone a fortune in having electric lights installed this far underground. As the flame caught, my eyes absorbed the light and quickly adjusted.

The heavy drapes were pulled over a window that looked out at nothing but sheer rock. My bathroom door was ajar and beside it was my desk. Several books were stacked there, one even still open, and there were some papers I'd been working on yesterday. A towel was draped over the back of my chair, but otherwise, there weren't any dirty clothes on the floor.

Because I had to wash them in the sink, I remembered darkly.

Cynthia and her minions had thrown blood on me. I could have *died*. Like, for real death. People thought vampires were already dead, that we had once been human and rose from the grave to… I don't know, terrorize the living or something stupid like that. It wasn't true. Vampires were born to vampire families, just like humans. Sure, we were allergic to sunlight and needed to drink blood to survive, but it wasn't like we slept in coffins or killed humans to sate our bloodlust.

I winced.

Okay, maybe we'd done that a time or two, but that was ages ago. Vampires were civilized now. Blood was taken from animals or synthesized in large underground vats. We weren't the monsters humans believed us to be.

Sighing, I tried to shove away thoughts of humans—like the ones carrying torches in my dreams, chasing me into the rising sun—or of the vampires here at school who apparently didn't care if I died.

I snorted. "I guess *some* of us are monsters."

Heading to the bathroom, I shoved aside my ruined uniform from the previous day and got into the shower. I washed my hair—twice, to make sure there wasn't any blood left—then got out to dress. There wasn't a mirror in the bathroom because I couldn't see my reflection anyway, but sometimes, I really wanted to know.

Did I really look so different from everyone else? There was only one way to know for sure and that was to find a pure silver looking-glass. Not exactly easy. There were rumors that the Ambrose family had one, which was why Dahlia always looked so perfect, but I kind of doubted it. You just didn't find silver looking-glasses anymore.

When I'd done my best, I stuffed several books into my bag and headed out toward dinner. It was still early, but the sun had officially gone down, so I figured there would be food by now. I thought about stopping to check on Corrine, but decided against it. Her trial was last night, and I didn't want to bug her about it, just in case it was difficult or something. She'd come find me when she was ready to talk about it.

After grabbing oatmeal—yes, vamps ate real food too—and my required morning blood, I went in search of a seat. Thankfully, it was early enough that there were a lot still open. I picked one toward the back where there was a long window overlooking the forest. We didn't get to see outside all that often, so I wasn't about to miss an opportunity.

I ate in silence, watching as students began to filter in.

I was waiting for Corrine, hoping that she would spill her guts about the lofty and mysterious tradition of The Trials, but I had yet to spot her. More and more students were filing in, grabbing food, laughing, or waking up, but still no Corrine. After a while, it was clear that no one else was entering the cafeteria.

Frowning, I started to get up when I noticed the whispering. There were some glances thrown my way, which wasn't unusual, but as I passed a table of girls, I heard them mention Corrine. I froze and tried to listen in, but they quickly clammed up.

That's it, I need to find Corrine, I thought to myself. I had a bad feeling about all this.

I hurried toward the door, but before I could make it into the hall, none other than Alexandre stepped in front of me. I stopped quickly before I ran into him, but just barely. "Alexandre!"

"Alex, please," he said with a small smile.

Alex? As in, he wanted me to call him Alex? I couldn't believe it. I'd run into him three times in two days and he was actually *talking* to me like we were friends. This was all really weird and if I hadn't been so worried about Corrine...

Shaking my head, I said, "I have to go. Corrine isn't here and—"

He cut me off before I even had the chance to finish. "She isn't going to be."

I stared at him. "What?"

Taking a slow breath, he shoved his hands into the pockets of his trousers, briefly looking away from me. After a moment, he said, "She isn't going to be here. Your friend... well, she isn't coming back."

My brain tried to process his words, but was having difficulty. What was he talking about? I just saw Corrine. Yesterday. She was heading to her trials and—

Slowly, I caught up. Something went wrong. "Of course, she is," I heard myself saying anyway, stubborn, disbelieving. "She's just running late. I just need to check on her and—"

Again, he cut me off, this time with a surprisingly gentle hand on my shoulder. "Corrine isn't running late, Bronwyn. She failed her trial. She's exiled."

For a second, the world froze. My skin paled and my vision blurred as black spots formed in front of my eyes. Everything, the sounds of the cafeteria and my own breathing, seemed to be coming from far away. I felt myself leaning backward, air slipping through my hair and along my skin as gravity tried to pull me to the ground.

I was probably fainting, but it never got that far. Instead, a pair of strong hands grabbed me by the shoulders. Dimly, I was aware that it was Alex and that he was pulling me away from the sounds of the cafeteria. By the time I really came back to myself, blinking away the dark spots, we were moving quickly down the corridor. I didn't know where we were headed, but Alex had one arm wrapped firmly across my shoulders and his other hand gripped the arm closest to him.

"What..." I tried to ask, but my voice came out tiny. "She can't be gone."

I glanced at Alex, but he was looking ahead, his blue eyes darting around as though looking for something.

I tried again, this time shaking Alex off. "She can't be gone! Even... even if she failed her test—we're allowed a week! A week to say good-bye to loved ones and to get ready. To gather our belongings and... and... I didn't get to say good-bye!"

Alex had turned to face me and I could see lines of sympathy softly drawn on his face. He ran a hand through his dark hair, then he shook his head. "I'm sorry. But *no one* got to say good-bye to Corrine. Not even her family."

I stared at him, open-mouthed. "What?"

Corrine's family weren't very high up in the ranks of vampires. They had little influence and lived pretty basic lives. They worked at the butcher's shop, supplying a good sum of the blood used here at the school. But that didn't have any bearing on their right to say good-bye to their only daughter. It was a right *every* family was afforded. There were no exceptions.

"I'm sorry," he repeated.

"You're sorry?" I demanded, my voice rising slightly. "You're sorry? No one got to say good-bye to Corrine before she was exiled from the Klatch *forever!* But you're sorry. Well, that just makes it all better."

He reached for me, maybe to comfort me, maybe to shake me or something, but I jerked away from him. I was mad now. "How could the Klatch do this? How can they pretend that this is okay? What, so long as she isn't a *pretty* vamp they can do whatever they want to her? How can anyone think this is right?"

I barely noticed the nervous way Alex was looking around. I almost kept barreling on, getting out as much as I could, because there was no one else I was going to be able to talk to now. Corrine, my best and only friend, was gone. But before I got the chance, Alex shushed me. "You need to come with me. Now."

Without another word, he turned on his heel and headed down the hall. It was my burning need to yell at someone about how unfair all this was that had me following him.

Or maybe I had just realized that he was, right now, my only chance to not be alone anymore.

Alex dipped into a classroom and I followed. Inside, it was empty. He leaned against the long teacher's desk, facing me. I opened my mouth to say something, probably to yell at him again, when he cut me off.

"Things are dangerous right now, Bronwyn." His voice was deep and low and serious enough that I snapped my mouth shut and just stared at him.

Dangerous?

"I'm sorry about your friend, really I am," he told me, and I wanted to believe he was being honest, though I couldn't exactly say why. "But you need to stop worrying about Corrine. There's nothing you can do for her."

My chest felt heavy with hurt as some part of me acknowledged that I would never see her again, even as the rest of me rallied against the idea. I was supposed to at least get a good-bye. Biting back tears, I sucked in a quick breath and tried to speak with an even tone. I failed. "But why?"

Alex ran another hand nervously through his hair. "I told you. Things are dangerous. Corrine—" He broke off and shook his head. "Like I said, there's nothing you can do for her. What's done is done. But your trial is tonight, and you need to start thinking about that."

For the first time that night, I was reminded that I, too, was coming of age. Before dawn, I would meet with the Klatch and receive my own assignment.

I felt almost sick at the thought.

Yesterday, I'd been joking with Corrine. I'd been reminding her that no one got exiled anymore, that the trial would be simple. But now, she wasn't here, and I was left with the horrifying realization that exile was a very real possibility.

And if Corrine failed, how could I ever pass?

My body began to shake as I contemplated how quickly I would be removed from the school. From everything I'd ever known. Relegated to the woods and the human-populated lands beyond. The humans that would kill me as soon as they realized what I was. And they would, eventually.

"What's going on?" I finally asked, my voice little more than a mouse's whisper.

Alex pushed away from the desk and took a step closer to me. I could smell the soft scent of the soap that he used and the lingering tang of copper that we all seemed to carry with us. "Just trust me. You need to do whatever the Klatch asks of you. No matter what it is."

I frowned as another shiver ran through me. *No matter what it is?* "What happened to Corrine?"

Alex didn't answer. Instead, he said, "You need to be careful. And you need to do what the Klatch says. They *will* test you."

I was trying to make sense of what he was saying because it didn't seem like the normal warnings about the trial. Everyone went through them. Everyone had to do what the Klatch asked of them... but somehow, I had the sudden sickening feeling that what the Klatch was going to ask of me was going to be horrifying.

Swallowing, I suddenly really considered who I was standing there with. Alexandre Petrovic. His father was Dimitri Petrovic, one of the three families that ruled the Klatch. He was so far out of my league that it was a miracle they even allowed us to attend the same school. He shouldn't even be talking to me.

Which was what sparked that tendril of doubt.

Why is he looking out for me?

"Why should I trust you?" is what I ended up asking, though I hadn't really been planning to.

His handsome face flickered with hurt, like I'd honestly offended him or something. "I've got your best interests at heart."

I let out a laugh before I could think better of it. His lips pursed into a thin line and he folded his arms across his broad chest. I managed to temper the laughing, and said, "Whatever. Your family hates me just like the others do. Your father is Dimitri Petrovic, not exactly a firm supporter of the imperfectness of vampires."

It was a nasty truth. Although it was widely accepted that the most perfect of vampires had the pale-blond hair of the Ambrose family and the Petrovics were the less-desirable, dark-haired lineage, Dimitri Petrovic constantly supported the pure bloodlines treaties. He believed that we needed to live up to our full potential and that full potential shone through only in the most beautiful of vampires.

It was disgusting, really, and it meant that I was the least desirable vampire in the entire town.

For a second, it looked like my words had struck a chord with Alex. He looked momentarily angry, but a second later, the expression slipped away. He looked almost... defeated. Letting out a sigh, he dropped his arms down to his side and said, "I'm sorry. I know how my father is and... well, let's just say I don't share the Klatch's narrow beliefs."

I stared at Alex uncertainly as I acknowledged a small part of me that really wanted to believe him. Maybe it was because Corrine was gone—and Hades, did that hurt—and I didn't want to be alone, or maybe it was because he was so attractive, and I wanted to believe that he thought, somehow, that I was too... I didn't know, but I wanted to believe him.

That didn't mean that I did, however. "But we're not even friends."

He stepped closer to me again. I almost backed up, but didn't. "I'd like to be."

"What about Dahlia?" I blurted, wishing immediately that I could snatch the words right from the air.

He snorted. "Please. It's hardly a match made in Elysium."

My eyebrows shot up in surprise. I didn't miss the dismissiveness of his tone or the lack of care as we spoke about the woman he was Promised to. But before I could find the words to ask him about it or press anything more about his warnings, the door to the classroom opened. The both of us jumped, jerking toward the sound.

Ms. Lynthens, the Romanian Studies teacher, walked in. She was a petite little thing with black hair that was pulled back severely in an attempt to give her a little more authority. It didn't really work. Her eyebrows rose when she spotted us, then quickly narrowed. "I don't want to know what the two of you are doing here, so just go before I have to find out." With that, she shooed us with a wave of her long, delicate hand, and turned to the chalkboard behind her.

I glanced at Alex and his eyes met mine for a long moment. When Ms. Lynthens cleared her throat, our gazes dropped, and Alex headed toward the door. Once he was out of the room, I waited two seconds, then followed. I glanced in either direction for Alex, but he was rounding the corner and then he was gone.

Feeling suddenly uncertain about everything, I decided that I didn't care whether or not I was late for my first class today. I needed to at least look for Corrine.

I headed back to the dorms, ignoring a perfectly dolled-up Dahlia and one of the boys from yesterday who, thankfully, gave me a wide berth. When I reached Corrine's dorm, I knocked as hard as I could, then waited. Nothing. I tried again, but still no answer.

"Corrine!" I called, but there was only silence.

Finally, I tried the door. To my dismay, it opened. Unlocked. Corrine never would have left her door unlocked. I pushed the heavy wood open. The room inside was immaculate and utterly empty.

No clothing.
No drawings.
No textbooks.
No throw pillows.

Nothing at all that might suggest a young vampire girl lived there. I was about to step inside and search for some small sign of my best friend, but before I got the chance, Heldens appeared behind me.

"Miss Nightshade." Her voice was cold and unkind. "I believe you have class right now. I suggest you hurry there, lest you annoy *that* teacher as much as you have me."

Reluctantly, I left Corrine's dorm, wondering how it was possible that I lost her in just a single day.

Chapter Four

Classes were a blur that night. I didn't learn a single thing, I was sure, and if I took any notes, they were likely illegible. My mind was full of other things. Corrine was exiled for failing her task. My own trial was coming up in only hours. And amidst it all, Alexandre Petrovic was leaving me some cryptic warning of dangers to come.

How was I supposed to focus on algebra at a time like this?

By the time I was done for the day, I felt exhausted. It was worse because I knew that I wouldn't be getting a reprieve. My trial was that night, just before dawn, and suddenly, there was this very real possibility that I could fail epically.

That I could be exiled too.

Would that be so bad? I wondered silently to myself as I closed the door to my dorm room behind me. Only a single day ago, I'd have thought there was little worse in this world than exile. Part of me still thought that, but as I reevaluated my life, I couldn't help but notice how little of a life I had.

My only friend was exiled.

The other vamps didn't seem to care if they injured or even killed me.

And even if those two things *weren't* true, there was still the irrefutable fact that I would never fit in with my own kind.

"Maybe when I fail, I can find Corrine and we can live together," I whispered to my empty room. I was mostly kidding, but my shaking hands belied my nervousness. I couldn't shake the feeling that I was going to fail and be exiled just like Corrine.

Undoing my tie and then the buttons on my blouse, I thought of what it might be like to be banished from the Klatch. No community, no one to protect you. Your choices would be limited to living in the wild, dark woods surrounding the town or going to the human towns past the mountains.

Neither was a very good option.

Humans would eventually find out what you were and the woods? Well, there wasn't exactly a lot of daylight protection there.

I shed my clothes and stepped into the shower. My stomach was twisted up into knots, so there was no point going down to dinner. One of the teachers would probably scold me for it later, but I didn't care. My cravings were never as bad as the others' were, and I knew that I could survive twelve hours without blood pudding.

I scrubbed myself until I was pink but clean, then got out and wrapped up in a towel.

Picking out a plain black dress—typical attire for a Klatch meeting—I started to untangle my red hair. I couldn't help but remember Alex's warning. *Things are dangerous right now. You need to be careful. They will test you.*

"Why me?"

It was a question I should have asked him but didn't. Why was he warning *me*? Was it just because my meeting was tonight? Or was it something else? Was he just running around, giving out warnings to everyone? I snorted at the idea. *Probably not.* Alex was gorgeous, but not really big on playing dark and mysterious. He didn't have to.

As my hand caught on a snarl of red hair, it finally occurred to me.

"Because I don't fit in."

Vampires didn't have red hair. They didn't have freckles, not even the faint ones like mine. I was a freak and everyone knew it. The only reason I'd been tolerated even this long was because of my father. Malcom Nightshade. I didn't remember him other than what stories and descriptions I'd gleaned from others, but I knew he had been well respected. Right up until the day he disappeared.

But even he hadn't looked anything like me. He'd had blond hair, they said, and was one of the most handsome vampires out there.

Which made everyone wonder how it was possible to have a child like me. Naturally, blame fell on my mother. Except no one seemed to know who she was. My father refused to tell and while there were a couple of maybes—all married women now who declined to step forward if they were my mother—nothing conclusive had ever come about.

It was like I had no mother at all.

Fighting back the wave of tears that always came whenever I thought about *that*, I focused on getting dressed. I needed to calm down and prepare myself for the meeting.

"Do whatever they say," I muttered to myself, repeating Alex's words from earlier. They were ominous. You only said something like that if you knew that what they were going to say was horrible. I shuddered at the knowledge.

When I was finally dressed, I took a final, calming breath. Then I left for the Klatch.

⁂

The Klatch met aboveground in what looked to be an old glass greenhouse. There were half-dead plants lining the glass walls, ivy filling in what patches remained clear. There was a walkway set in stone down the center of the long house, and on either side of it was a slowly moving stream. I frowned at the sight of the moving water, knowing that it was there for a reason.

To make sure that I couldn't run.

Vampires couldn't cross moving water. The only way in or out of the greenhouse was where I'd just come from because the streams met up ahead in a gentle arch that effectively separated me from the three reigning members of the Klatch.

I walked as calmly as I could down the stone aisle and stopped in front of the stream. On the other side were three chairs made from rusted iron, wrapped in thick, blackened vines. On one side was Melicent Deskin, a beautiful, blonde-haired vampire. She was the only woman on the Klatch, and the cold look in her blue eyes told me that she was mean enough to have earned it. On the opposite side was Dimitri Petrovic. He looked down at me as though I were a bug that needed squashing. I wondered how someone like *that* could have had someone like Alexandre. They might have looked the same, but that was where the similarities ended.

I hoped.

Finally, sitting in the center, was Vincent Ambrose. His blond hair was combed back from his handsome face and his blue eyes looked sharp, if maybe a little bored at the whole ordeal. He was Dahlia's father and there was no questioning it. They could have been carbon copies of each other.

"Bronwyn Nina Nightshade," he addressed me, using my full name. "You have reached your Age of Becoming, and we welcome you to your Trial."

I swallowed heavily. For a moment, my mouth was so dry that I thought I wouldn't be able to say anything in return. That I was going to mess this whole thing up and they would not only laugh at me, but throw me out into exile without ever even bothering to give me a task.

Ambrose raises a delicate eyebrow at me, waiting for some sort of acknowledgment.

Choking a little, I managed to get out, "Thank you. It is my honor."

I thought I saw Deskin actually roll her eyes at me, but I couldn't be sure because I wasn't willing to look away from Ambrose for more than a couple of seconds. He was that intimidating.

"There are rules of your Trial, Child of the Night," said Ambrose in a deadly serious tone. "First, you must speak to no one of it. You may ask for no assistance and none may offer it to you. You must vow your silence." He paused, waiting for me.

I stumbled over my words to get them out fast enough. "I vow my silence, on my honor."

"Second," he continued, not even acknowledging my response. "You have only one week to complete your task. By the dawn of the seventh day, we must have proof of your success." He waited again.

"By the seventh dawn," I repeated.

"The third is this. If you fail in your task, you will be exiled. Banished from this world forever, and should you dare to return, the punishment can only be death." His voice seemed to drop even lower on the word *death*, sending it straight through my very bones.

I swallowed heavily. "I will not fail," I murmured, barely loud enough for them to hear.

Ambrose nodded his head in acknowledgment, then he sat up straighter. "Very well. Bronwyn Nightshade, I give to you your task." There was a long, thoughtful pause. Almost like he didn't already have this all worked out and was making up my task on the spot. For a bright moment, I thought it really *was* going to be something stupid like picking wildflowers from the woods. Then he spoke and all my hopes disintegrated. "To drain a human of their blood."

Shock slipped through me like a knife. I must have heard wrong. "I'm s-sorry," I stuttered, wide-eyed. "What did you say?"

Petrovic glared down at me, even more annoyed with my presence than before. "Drain a human of their blood. You have one week's time to do so, Nightshade. If you fail, you bring disgrace and exile to yourself." He paused a moment, then a slow smile spread across his mouth. It made his lips look smaller and his face stretch awkwardly in the light. "And to your father."

My spine straightened instantly. The threat toward my father wasn't about his life or exile. He was already dead. But his memory was all I had left, and if I failed, they'd take that from me too. They'd smear his name and disown his reputation. All because I'd failed.

But they can't be serious, I thought, searching for some sign of joking amidst their severe faces.

There was none.

Vampires didn't drink from humans. Mostly. Yes, there was always some rogue out there, doing bad things and giving us all a bad name, but most of us just weren't like that. We had synthetic blood and animal blood to survive on. Hunting humans... it was a thing of the past. Barbaric. Savage. Inhumane.

And yet I was standing here in the greenhouse, staring up at the Klatch, aware that they had just given me an undeniable order. Failure was to lose everything, and refusal was failure.

"B-but we don't feed on humans," I murmured weakly, still searching for an explanation. This had to be a test.

Petrovic looked down his nose at me, curling his upper lip in a sneer. "You do whatever we tell you to do. That's how this works. Our trial is absolute. You have no say—unless you'd like to forfeit now and begin your exile immediately."

I didn't say anything.

Petrovic smiled at my silence. "As I suspected. Now, leave. You're dismissed. Remember your task—and keep your silence. To speak of this is to fail."

I was completely numb. How had I stumbled into this little glass house and walked into another world completely? Because this one couldn't be mine. Not with orders to kill and promises of destroying my father's good name. This was all supposed to be easy. To be a breeze. A little trial to prove that I was just like everyone else, and then go on with my life.

But this?

I turned to leave, having been dismissed, but something made me pause. *Unless you'd like to begin your exile immediately.*

My mind drifted to Corrine, my one real friend, and how she'd been exiled without so much as a good-bye. Had she failed immediately? And if she had, was it because she'd been given the same task I had?

A shiver ran down my spine.

If Corrine had been given this task and refused, was it possible that *everyone* was given this task? The thought turned my stomach to rot. I didn't want to believe it because it meant that everyone over seventeen... was a murderer.

Including Alex.

His handsome face appeared in my head, and I had to shove it aside because, suddenly, it was dripping with blood and his eyes were black with hunger.

I swiveled back around to face the Klatch. They'd begun to mumble amongst themselves already, and I should have just left it at that, but my mouth was working before I could think better of it. "Is this why Corrine failed?"

As soon as the words were out, I wished I could snatch them back. The members of the Klatch each turned their eyes upon me, staring with surprised—and angry—gazes. They didn't like my question. They didn't like that I'd asked it at all.

I swallowed heavily.

It was Ambrose who spoke. "Corrine Lace is exiled. She is no longer ours and we do not speak of those that are not ours. I never wish to hear that name again." He actually bared his teeth at me.

I stumbled several steps back, mumbling an apology. Then, before anyone could get angrier, I turned and ran like my life depended on it. Maybe it did.

Chapter Five

The clock was ticking. I had only a week to complete my task, and if I didn't, that would be it. I'd be exiled. Banished from everything I knew, left to the wild woods or the human cities. Neither was a good prospect given my vampiric nature. But could I really kill a human? Did they honestly expect that of me?

"This has to be a test," I muttered to my ceiling.

I was lying on my bed in my dorm room. It was daylight outside, so everyone was in their dorms, sleeping. But I couldn't sleep. Only hours earlier, I'd been ordered to drain a human dry. Any human. Not that I'd ever seen one. The nearest human was in the Romanian town of Transylvania. Not exactly a hop, skip, and a jump from here. The only way to even get there was to hike through the woods to the rail station. It was several miles away and there were no vehicles between here and there.

But it wasn't the inconvenience of it all that turned my stomach. It was the idea of killing someone. Not an animal, but an actual human—a person, like me. Or sort of like me. Obviously, there were fundamental differences between our kinds.

Little things like being allergic to sunlight and needing blood to sustain ourselves.

I snorted. "Yeah, little differences."

And that was when I realized that I wasn't just hesitant because I didn't want to kill something that looked and thought like I did. I was scared because *they* might kill *me*. If they found out what I was.

"Maybe I can blend," I murmured.

I tugged at a red curl of hair, pulling the strand around so that it was in front of my face where I could see it. Without a mirror, it was difficult to know if I looked human enough to pass. But I had color in my hair, and Corrine always said I got color in my cheeks when I was embarrassed. But was that enough to be considered human?

Everyone else thinks so, I thought to myself.

That wasn't exactly true, but those girls had all but accused me of being human. Or at least of not being a real vampire. Maybe, for once, that would work in my favor.

I sighed, letting my hair drop back onto my pillow. "I can't do this."

Drain a human. Kill a human. Remove all their blood and present proof of their death to the Klatch. And do it all in a week. I wasn't even sure if I could find a human in a week, much less kill one. And even if I could...

I sat up abruptly and threw my legs over the side of the bed. This was crazy. Vamps couldn't just go around killing people. That was how you got Hungers and Van Helsings and everything else out there who wanted to skewer us. Seriously, it was a *rule*. Well, sort of. No killing humans—unless they stumbled upon the Klatch, but that was for our own protection too. And, okay, it was technically all right to feed from humans, so long as you didn't get caught, but...

I was starting to realize that our rules were all about protecting us and not in the least bit concerned about killing someone else.

Standing, I began to pace around my small dorm room. Part of me knew that I should get some sleep, rest up for whatever was to come, but I couldn't make myself tired enough. I was wired from the meeting, and my thoughts wouldn't give me a break. The idea of murder just kept wandering round and round in my head, chasing exile and Corrine until I felt completely exhausted and utterly unable to sleep.

I chewed at my lower lip.

"Maybe exile isn't so bad," I mumbled. "Corrine's my only friend anyway, and if she's exiled, maybe we can be exiled together."

Even as I tried to convince myself of how this all might work out for the best, a cold knot formed in my stomach. Exile was terrifying. It was giving up everything I ever knew and trying to survive in a world that seemed well equipped to kill my sorry little vamp butt. And even if Corrine was out there, there was no guarantee that I'd find her.

What if I spent the rest of my probably short life alone?

I shuddered at the thought. The only thing that had made life bearable thus far was the knowledge that I hadn't had to spend it alone. No, I didn't have family and most of the other vamps hated or ignored me, but I wasn't *alone*. Corrine was there for me, and now I had Alex—

I abruptly stopped pacing, catching myself. "Whoa. I do *not* have Alex. He's... he's not mine. He's a friend. An acquaintance, really."

Heat rose to my cheeks, probably turning them pink. I shouldn't have even thought of Alex, but I couldn't help but remember how he suddenly seemed to be talking to me. Or how he'd gone out of his way to warn me. How he'd been the only one who cared enough to even tell me about Corrine.

I frowned. Had Alex known about the trial? He was seventeen already and his father was a member of the Klatch. Was it possible that Alex had been asked to kill a human too? And worse, was he still here because he *had*?

A shudder ran down my spine. I wanted to push the thoughts from my head, but they wouldn't go.

"I need out of this room."

I went to the door, hesitating only for a moment. It was still daylight outside, so everyone was supposed to stay in their dorms, at least until dusk. But all of the halls on this floor were underground and the drapes upstairs would be drawn anyway. It wasn't as though it was dangerous. And besides, it wasn't like I had classes or anything else to worry about. If I ended up awake all day and asleep late into the night, well, I wouldn't be missing much of anything.

After rationalizing it to myself, I swung the door open and stepped out into the hall. I poked my head out first, glancing in either direction to see if anyone else was up. When it looked clear, I stepped out into the hall and started walking.

I wasn't really sure where I was headed, I just needed out of that room. Somewhere to think, to figure out what I was going to do about all this.

It wasn't until I was standing outside of Corrine's door that I realized where my feet had taken me. My heart ached, knowing that she wasn't on the other side. I really could have used her to talk to.

Glancing around me once more, I reached for the doorknob. I expected it to be locked, hoped it would be, and that all this was just a bad dream... but it wasn't. The knob turned easily in my hand, and I pushed the door open. Inside was just a room.

Just like before, the room was bare. It was set up like all the dorm rooms before someone moved in. A bed tucked in the corner. A desk on the opposite wall. A nightstand and a door leading to a bathroom. A closet—

Frowning, I stepped farther into the room, moving toward the closet. It was half open, and as I stared at it dumbly, I remembered something. A secret between only Corrine and me.

"I'm not stupid," *Corrine told me indignantly.* "I know Heldens would never let me keep it."

She was wrapping the book up in a red silk cloth like she might a present. Then she wound some twine around the middle of it and tied a sloppy bow.

"So what are you doing?" *I asked, nodding toward the book. It was just a book, and normally, it wouldn't be a big deal for Corrine to have it. But it was one of about ten books that we weren't allowed to have. If anyone found it, she'd be in trouble. If Heldens found it, she'd get a year's worth of it.*

"Duh, I'm hiding it."

She smiled at me, her cheeks plump, and her eyes large. She hopped off her bed where we'd been sitting, and I watched as she moved to the closet door. Sending me a wink, she yanked open the door to reveal her clothes. Mostly, they were school uniforms, but she had a couple of other things too. Jeans, T-shirts, a dress her mother had made her for a dance she never went to. At the bottom were shoes and several boxes filled with knickknacks and generally useless things that Corrine loved to collect.

But she wasn't going to put the book there with that collection. Instead, she reached her hand into the hanging clothes and shoved them back. Behind the fabric was a wall of bricks, just like in all the other rooms.

"What are you—" I shut up as I saw her fingers feel along the edges of several bricks before settling on one in particular.

She moved her pointer finger along the outline of the brick, then dug her nails beneath it. Perfect. She grinned as she yanked the brick out to reveal a small compartment. It already had several things in there, parchment and some drawing utensils that were her favorites. A ring and a bracelet. She put the book in there, too, and told me, "No one knows about it. Just me—and now you."

And now me.

I'd forgotten all about it because she'd only shown me the one time. That was almost two years ago. But as I stood there in her barren room, I realized that if it really had been a secret, then her stash of trinkets was still there.

Desperate for anything of hers, anything that might have belonged to my best friend, I dove for the closet. Pushing the door open the rest of the way, I stared at the brick wall. Each brick looked just like the last, and I wasn't sure which one had been her hiding spot, but I decided that I'd check all of them to find something of hers.

My fingers began to trail over the grout between the bricks, searching for something loose or something that felt different.

Brick after brick was nothing. Just that, a brick. I was about to give up when I felt something shift beneath my fingertip. *This is it!* Eager, I dug at the grout. My nails caught on the edges of the brick and with a soft, grinding sound, I managed to wiggle the brick from its hole.

I smiled and eagerly looked inside, hoping to find all her little trinkets. Instead, I found an empty hole. This, too, had been cleaned out. My shoulders slumped as disappointment washed through me. I'd been so sure...

I stuck my hand into the hole, letting it smooth around in the darkness, just to make sure that it really was empty. *No book, no art supplies, no jewelry or—*

My hand froze when it stumbled over something. Soft and smooth, my fingers eagerly wrapped around it and yanked it out. I jerked it out quickly and as a result, pulled something else along with it. It made a clanking sound as it hit the floor. Frowning, I bent down to retrieve it. *A ring*. It was the one I'd seen in there before and excitement flared again.

It was Corrine's!

The other thing, the thing I'd felt initially, was crumpling in my hand. A piece of parchment. I opened it up and smoothed it out to reveal that it was a drawing. Of me and Corrine. My heart clenched as I stared down at the only picture I had of her. We didn't show up on film or anything, so it was impossible to capture our likenesses unless you could draw. Corrine could and it showed here. I'd had to describe her as best I could, and it took her days to get anything close to accurate, but eventually she'd managed. It wasn't perfect, but it looked like her.

I plopped down heavily on the bare mattress, holding the ring and the picture. Unable to look at the picture of my best friend anymore without thinking of exile and my terrible task, I flipped it over onto the mattress. That was when I saw that something was written on the back.

My brow furrowed as I picked the parchment back up to study the scrawling handwriting. It was Corrine's.

I you have this, I've failed. And it means you're next. Find the Harker before your time is up.

—Corrine

I stared at it. "What?" I knew Corrine better than just about anyone, maybe even her own parents, but I couldn't make heads or tails of the message on the back. Failed could have meant her task—it probably did, as a matter of fact. And me next? Well, I did have my trial right after her and I—

Well, I was probably going to fail too.

But what did "find the Harker" mean? What in Hades was a Harker?

I didn't know, but if she hid it in a place only I could find, then it had to be important. And it had to be for me.

I stayed in Corrine's room for a while after that, just staring at the message and holding the ring in my open palm. I might have stayed there all day if I hadn't heard someone coming down the hall. Panicked, I shoved the ring on my finger, the drawing in my back pocket, and the brick back in place. Then I darted into the closet myself, hiding as I listened for the sound again. I heard footsteps and worried that they'd come in here. They paused right outside the door for a second, and I was sure I was caught, but then I heard the door pulled shut. The footsteps started again and whoever it was disappeared down the hall.

I gave it ten minutes, then I ran from the room and went back into my own room. I still didn't sleep much that day, but I didn't leave my room again. Instead, I read that message another thousand times.

By dusk, I'd promised myself that I would find whatever this Harker was, no matter what.

Chapter Six

That night found me in the library. I was increasingly aware of the clock ticking away toward my failure and subsequent exile, but I still wasn't sure that I could make myself take a human life. No matter what.

I had the drawing folded up and stuffed down into my bra for safekeeping because I doubted anyone was going to look there anytime soon. But now that I was in the library, alone, I pulled it out and unfolded it to set beside the open book on the table. Since I didn't have classes, I at least had some time to really get working on my problem.

The one where I either had to kill someone or be exiled, but also the riddle at the back of Corrine's picture. Maybe the two things weren't related, but the more I thought about it, the more I was sure that they were.

She had failed, which meant exile.

I was scheduled for my trial right after her. I would fail too.

And something about a Harker.

It was that last part that I was trying to figure out. Corrine's message had told me to find it, but I wasn't even sure what it was. Thus, the library.

Twirling Corrine's ring around my finger—I'd put it on to keep it safe, but also because it reminded me of her—I flipped the page in the large tomb laid out on the table in front of me. It weighed about a thousand pounds and read like dust, but I needed a place to start and this was as good as any.

It was a reference book for important objects in Vampiric Lore. My least favorite subject, which was why I thought maybe I hadn't heard of a Harker before.

I was reading about whimsicals, which were musical instruments used in Europe to chase off vampires. Although we'd worked hard to get them off the books as far as humans were concerned, they were actually effective. The sound they created could make our ears bleed until we died, or distract and disorient us long enough that the sun could come up or we could be staked. Or burned alive.

"Can't forget burned alive," I muttered under my breath.

There were like three more pages about whimsicals, and I was bored out of my mind when the door to the library opened. I jerked my head up and slammed the book closed at the same time, even though whimsicals didn't have anything to do with Harkers—as far as I could tell—and no one would know what I was doing anyway.

Coming into the library was none other than Dahlia, her beautiful blonde hair falling past her shoulders like a sheet of glasslike golden water. Her crystalline blue eyes fixed on me and my bumbling efforts to hide my research instantly.

Tilting her head to the side curiously, she walked toward me.

Please keep going, please keep going...

Dahlia hadn't ever been mean to me. At least, not directly. A lot of vamps hadn't. But she was the prettiest vampire in the school—even compared to the boys, though I was willing to argue that Alex was more handsome at least—and that meant she was definitely not in my sphere. Which meant that her talking to me basically meant trouble.

Pretty vampires didn't talk to me without an agenda, and usually that was to make me utterly miserable. And after that whole incident with the other girls, it was hard not to worry. In fact, it was downright impossible.

I was hoping that she really would just keep walking to wherever she was headed. It was a legitimate possibility because we really didn't have any interactions before this, but—

"You're not in class."

She delicately folded herself up into the chair adjacent to mine, sitting at the corner of the table.

My eyes went wide. "Um—" I struggled for a full minute to find a suitable lie before I realized that the *truth* was actually the best way to go this time. "I don't have classes this week. I just turned seventeen."

She smiled at me, her lips forming a perfect pink slice out of her mouth. Her eyes were so large in her head that she looked like a strange, living doll. The smile made that twice as creepy. "That's right. I forgot about that." She put her elbows on the table and leaned forward, folding her hands up beneath her chin to rest it on. "You're starting your trial, aren't you?"

I nodded. My palms began to sweat and I moved them off the table to discreetly rub them on the skirt of my uniform. *Why am I even wearing the uniform today? I don't have class.*

"So... what was your task?"

Her voice was little more than a whisper and her smile told me that this was a secret, but my eyes still went wide, and I stared at her like she'd lost her mind. I looked around for someone who might have heard us, but it was just the two of us here in the library.

"Y-you know I can't tell you that."

She laughed a little, sitting back in her chair and waving one of her hands around like she could swat my words away. "Oh, don't be such a worry wart. Everyone talks about their tasks, they just don't, you know, *talk* about them. We keep it quiet, you know?"

I bit my lip, not sure if she was just messing with me or if she was being honest. Was I just so devoid of friends that no one told me about their tasks? *Maybe*, I conceded. Corrine had been my only friend, and she hadn't had the chance to tell me her task, so maybe...

Clearing my throat, I tried to smile. It felt brittle in my mouth. "Um, oh. Well. I don't think I should—"

Her full mouth pulled together into a frown. Even then, she looked stunningly beautiful, if a little odd. I thought she was going to push harder on the subject, but instead, she interrupted me with, "What's going on with you and Alex?"

My jaw dropped before I could help it. Heat rose steadily to my cheeks and my eyes were so wide that I thought they were going to fall out of my head. *Oh, god. This is not good.* "Um....... . We..." I had no idea how to answer that until I realized the truth: there wasn't anything going on with Alex. At most, he'd said he wanted to be friends and even that was tentative. In the end, I wasn't even in the nearby sphere of maybe being able to threaten her in some way, shape, or form.

I couldn't explain why that upset me a little bit. It wasn't as though I'd expected anything from Alex, and yet...

Snapping my jaw closed, I cleared my throat, then said, "Nothing. We just... talk sometimes." It sounded lame, even to my own ears, but it was the truth.

Dahlia let out a sigh. "Pity." She sounded legitimately disappointed.

I stared at her in confusion. "What?"

She lifted a single delicate shoulder, her fine blonde hair slipping off it like silk. "It's just that Alex is so *boring*, you know?"

No, I didn't know that. In fact, he seemed very interesting to me, especially after his little warning the other night. But I kept my mouth shut and let Dahlia do all the talking.

"He's hardly the sort of person I want to spend the rest of my life with. I was thinking that this"—she gestured toward me—"would at least make him a little more interesting." She rolled her eyes. "That's what I get for hoping. He's too straight and narrow for that. Boring. Completely boring. I mean, how am I supposed to live a supremely interesting life full of adventure if my supposed partner in crime is this by-the-books vamp boy toy?"

She looked at me then, her eyes wide, her delicate eyebrows raised, and her hands held out, palms up. Like she expected me to just completely understand where she was coming from. But I didn't. I lived a pretty pathetic existence normally, but after having a little adventure injected into that existence, I would trade just about anything to go back to it. Between murder and exile, I'd already had enough adventure in my life—and I'd only had that for a day.

When I only stared silently at Dahlia in response, she sighed and let her hands drop. She rolled her eyes and said, "Never mind."

I felt bad for not understanding, but could she really blame me for not grasping this concept that Alexandre Petrovic was boring?

Changing the subject, she leaned over the table and reached for the heavy book. She drew it to her before I could even think to stop her. *Wow, she's fast.* "What are you doing?"

"Nothing," I said as quickly as I could get out.

I reached for the book to pull it back, but that was a big mistake. It just drew attention to the drawing I'd left unfolded on the table when Dahlia had come to join me.

Her bright blue eyes fastened on it, excitement shining in them. "Ooh, what's this?"

I tried to grab hold of it, but once again, she reached for it and had it in her hands before I could even blink. She was so much faster than me. Most vamps were, unfortunately.

She studied the picture of me and Corrine and I hoped she wouldn't see the message on the other side. Maybe I could play it off as a souvenir since I didn't get to say good-bye to Corrine. Or maybe something I had from awhile back that—

Then she flipped the page over. "A message?" As she read, her already large eyes grew wider. "Oh my god! This is, like, a quest! Is this your task?"

I snatched the page from her hands and tucked it down my shirt. She raised an eyebrow at this, but didn't comment. Instead, she said, "Is that what you're doing in here? Looking for where to find the Harker?"

I was about to tell her to leave me alone, that this was private, when I noted how she said it. *The Harker*. Like... like maybe she knew what it was. Hope blossomed in my chest. I was having no luck and didn't even know what I was really looking for. If she knew, then maybe I could cut straight to the chase. Biting my lip, I debated for a second more, then asked, "Do you know what it is?"

She blinked at me. "What what is?"

Exasperated, I said, "The *Harker*."

She gave me a look. "I assumed it was one of the Harkers. You know, the Van Helsing's Harker."

"What are you talking about?"

"You know, the Van Helsings that Heldens is always going on about. The original Vampire Hunting Family. Those that kill together, stay together, and all that."

I waved her on with my hand. "I know about the Van Helsings. But what does that have to do with a Harker?"

"Don't you pay attention in history?" When I just stared at her—clearly, I didn't—she sighed and explained. "The Harkers were a second family of Hunters. Like the Van Helsings, they claimed to have lost one of their own 'to the darkness' as humans like to say. They were friends with the Van Helsings, or something like that, and together they fought our kind."

My shoulders slumped. That was not the answer that I'd been hoping for. "Then that doesn't help at all."

"It doesn't?"

I shook my head. "How could it? If they're Hunters with the Van Helsings, then they're all dead too. Meaning there's not a Harker to find."

Dahlia grinned at me, shaking her head a little. "Wrong. While the Van Helsings died out, the Harkers supposedly survived. The Harkers gave up the hunt and just became boring old scholars. I mean, how do you give up a life of adventure for a library?" She gestured to the stacks of books surrounding us.

She continued to berate the lifestyle choices of the Harkers, but I wasn't really listening. If she was right and the Harker name survived, then was it possible that Corrine was talking about one of them? She'd said *the* Harker, like there was one in particular. Was it because there was only one left or just a specific one to find?

And if she did want me to find a person, not a thing, then the question changed: Why?

Feeling frustrated, I sighed and forced myself to thank Dahlia. Even though I wasn't sure it helped, I at least had an idea of what Corrine's message had been referring to. "Thanks for your help."

I started to gather up my things, writing off essentially every book I'd grabbed from the shelves. None of them would tell me anything about the Harker family. But before I could leave, Dahlia reached out and grabbed my arm.

"Wait! You're just leaving?"

I shrugged a little. "Well, yeah. I have to figure things out."

She stood abruptly, still holding my arm. "What about me?"

I blinked at her. "What about you?" I winced, realizing that sounded kind of bad. "I just mean, this doesn't really have anything to do with you. Corrine left that message for me."

She flapped her delicate hand around in the air as though waving off Corrine's very memory. "Who cares about that? You clearly need some help and this is really important. I have to assume—since you won't tell me outright—that this has to do with your trial. Well, I can help with that, obviously."

Dahlia Ambrose had absolutely no idea what she was talking about. She couldn't possibly understand that my trial was to drain a human dry; that Corrine had failed her trial, and I was betting it was because her task had been the same, or that she'd left me this cryptic message because Corrine had failed already. She kept talking about this great adventure like it was a game, but this was *my life*. Dahlia had already gone through her task. She was over seventeen. But she didn't understand the urgency for me.

This could destroy my life. Or maybe even worse.

I opened my mouth to tell her that much, but she leaned forward, her huge, doll-like eyes practically glistening.

"If you're going on some adventure, I want to come too."

I shook my head and flatly said, "No." I tried to pull my arm free, but she held tightly to it. She wouldn't let me go so easily, and for the first time since she'd sat down with me, I was honestly nervous.

"Let me put this another way," she said in a sickly sweet voice. "Either you let me in on this, or I tell the Klatch about this picture and its message."

I felt a flash of anger, but I knew better than to do anything about it. Dahlia was faster and likely stronger than me. Most vamps were. And if I were being really honest about things? I didn't want to do this alone anyway.

So I did the only thing I could. I said, "Okay."

Chapter Seven

We were holed up in my dorm room. It was weird to see Dahlia lounging on my bed, looking like some ethereal, underworld goddess. I told her that she didn't have to follow me around; I would tell her whenever I figured something out. But she didn't believe me. Which told me that she was smarter than I gave her credit for.

"You're really not going to tell me what your trial is?"

This was the tenth time she'd asked me this question in the last hour. I'd considered telling her, but I was torn between this notion that only *I* was given this horrible task and *everyone* was given this task. Both of these things seemed bad. And I just wasn't sure that I could be in the same room with Dahlia knowing that she'd killed someone.

So I shoved the possibility aside and focused on the message. It all had to be tied up together.

"No, Dahlia. I'm not going to tell you."

She shrugged her shoulders. "Fine. I'm just saying, if all of this is linked"—she waved at the parchment crinkled on my bedspread—"then I should have all the details before we embark."

And cue second frustration.

I rounded on Dahlia, putting my hands on my hips. "Embark where? We don't even know where to start looking for this Harker, whoever he or she is."

Sitting up suddenly, her pouty lips lifting in an eager smile, she said, "That's not true. We definitely know where to start. It's in our history."

I raised an eyebrow at her, waiting for her explanation.

"Transylvania. It's the nearest town anyway, and we'd have to stop there even if we were going farther, you know? But that's where all the Hunting was supposed to take place back before the Klatch was founded and we started the school. I'll bet their family still lives there."

"Assuming they haven't all died out," I muttered.

Dahlia ignored me and I silently admitted to myself that she had a pretty valid point. I'd been thinking that I would have to go to Transylvania anyway. Whether it would be to kill and drain a human or to search for a safe place to live out the remainder of my lonely, miserable existence, I wasn't sure, but Dahlia was right about that at least. It was the place to go.

"Won't you be missed?" I finally asked Dahlia. I was exempt from classes this week; she was not.

She waved off my concerns. "Don't worry about it. My father's head of the Klatch right now, remember? I'll just wave a little note at Heldens and be done with it."

I frowned. On some level, yes, she was definitely right. On the other side of it, though, this was a little different than just skipping class. This was leaving the safety of the Klatch and going to a town that was full of humans. And probably taking enough time there that we'd have to spend the day in hiding.

"Yeah, but won't your parents worry?"

Obviously, Vincent Ambrose was both Dahlia's father and leader of the Klatch. I liked him less than I liked blood. Her mother, however, was in the limelight a lot less. Cordelia Ambrose was just as lovely as Dahlia, but twice as fragile. She seemed constantly sickly, though the Ambrose family denied it at every turn. They said that she was just paler than most, or thinner than most. If anything, by vampire standards, this made her more ideal than anyone else.

But the rumors persisted. Surely, that sickly mother would miss her only daughter.

Dahlia's face went completely blank. Her features were slack, her mouth in a neutral line, her large eyes glassy. She really looked like a doll in that moment and it creeped me out. "My parents won't even notice I'm gone." Her tone was as blank and emotionless as her face.

I felt like there was something there, something I should ask about, but what? I didn't know anything about family dynamics, so it really wasn't my place to ask.

"Okay, well..." I didn't have any more arguments, and if I was being perfectly honest with myself, I didn't want to convince her to stay. Going to Transylvania by myself was terrifying. "I guess we need to pack."

Her face lit up with excitement. Animated once more, she hopped off the bed and threw open my closet like it was her own. "You need to dress trendy if we're actually going somewhere."

"I was just going to take my uniform."

She swiveled around to face me, a look of utter disbelief on her face. "Are you crazy?"

I felt my cheeks begin to warm and looked away. I headed to my bed and knelt down beside it to reach beneath the mattress. My luggage was stashed there, though I hadn't had to use it in years. People like Dahlia could go home to their families for holidays and things, but I stayed here year round. Since my father was dead and my mother was unknown, I was technically a ward of the Klatch. The school was as much my home as anywhere else.

Which was part of the reason I was so embarrassed that Dahlia was digging through my closet.

I didn't have a lot of clothes that weren't my school uniform. What I did have came as a gift from Corrine.

"It's not that big of a deal, Dahlia," I muttered, pulling out my suitcase.

"Of course it is! I'm sure you have something decent in here that you can pack."

Letting out a sigh, I let her dig through my clothes. I had the feeling there was no stopping her on this one. She tossed article after article out of my closet and onto my bed. A shirt hit me in the face when her aim was wrong. She didn't even apologize.

"Like this!"

She held out a sparkly black dress that Corrine's mom had given her in the hopes that she would lose enough weight to wear it. That hadn't happened. In fact, Corrine had been so upset about the whole thing, that she'd thrown it at me, ordered me to try it on, and insisted that I keep it forever and ever. I told her not to pawn off her mother's rude gifts to me, but she softened and promised that the dress looked awesome on me.

I'd never had a reason to wear it, but I kept it in my closet.

"Are we going to find this Harker guy—or girl, whatever—or are we going to some underworld party?" I demanded, standing up and snatching the dress from her.

She rolled her eyes. "Don't be a snot. We should dress to impress. Or at least to look more like the humans."

"And the humans don't have schoolgirls?"

She shrugged her shoulder and took the dress back from me. Then she threw it into the bottom of my suitcase before turning back to look through the rest of my closet. Apparently, she deemed the matter was closed. I thought about trying to sneak it out of the suitcase again, then decided it wasn't that big of a deal. It was just a stupid dress, and I probably wouldn't even pull it out of the bottom of that suitcase anyway.

In the end, Dahlia picked out another dress—this one a white button-down that had long sleeves—and then scrounged up some leather pants that I hadn't worn in a long time. Didn't have much reason to. I added in a complete uniform, much to her chagrin, and some leggings. All I had to do was grab a coat, my shoes, and my shoulder bag (because I wasn't going to drag my suitcase around with me everywhere).

I was about to tell Dahlia to go pack, too, but she grabbed my arm and dragged me away before I had the chance.

"Now, we'll pick out *my* clothes and I'll show you how it's done."

※

It was done by taking *hours* to decide on the perfect outfit. I was so sick of looking at clothing that I was contemplating gouging out my own eyes. It was nearly midnight when she was finally packed and ready to go. I could have throttled her for it because it meant that we wouldn't have as much darkness to make it through the woods to reach the station, but Dahlia wasn't concerned.

"I know the quickest way through the woods."

"How?" I asked her as we carried out suitcases toward the main entrance to the school.

She just smiled prettily and sent me a wink. "Don't worry about it."

It turned out that Dahlia was right though. She *did* know the quickest way through the woods. As vampires, we didn't travel outside the safety of our little village very often. We didn't have reason to, and since it was so dangerous, most opted against it.

Unless they were exiled.

Just like I'm going to be.

We picked our way along a barely-there footpath. It looked like it was used on occasion, but clearly not enough to really be considered a deliberate path. It was more like "This is the easiest way through the forest, so everyone happens to walk here." Which was okay with me. I was constantly struggling to catch up with Dahlia who moved so much faster than I did.

"Why are you so slow?" she commented for the third time in about two hours.

I was panting behind her, pushing my hands to the tops of my thighs in an effort to shove off. I didn't know where the other vamps got their energy from because it seemed like I was constantly lacking.

No wonder they all joke that I'm human.

"Shut up," I told her rudely.

She just shrugged her shoulders, unconcerned, then waited at the top of yet another hill for me to catch up. It took me a minute, but eventually, I managed it.

"How far is the station exactly?"

A human averaged about three miles an hour if they walked constantly at a normal pace. A vampire did about three or four times that without breaking a sweat. If they ran, it was faster still.

Me? I was lucky if I did twice that, and I was winded at the end of it.

Which was why I was sucking in air like a bagpipe. We'd been walking for just over two hours, and the entire way it had been uphill. Dahlia set a brutal pace that I couldn't keep up with, so she was always complaining about going so slow, but that was the best I could do.

If I had to guess, we'd covered at least twelve miles. I hoped.

She looked over the side of the hill then back at me. A smile graced her lips. "Not too long now. Look."

I forced myself to straighten up and look down the side of the hill. Thank Hades, the station was right there! Granted, *right there* happened to be another four or five miles of walking, but at least it would be downhill.

Finally, I was catching a break.

"C'mon! Let's get going. The sun'll be up in a few hours."

That sent a chill down my spine. I knew what sunlight did to vampires and it wasn't good. Picking up the pace, I didn't quite match Dahlia, but I was doing better. We made it to the station in just over an hour. I was exhausted, but we beat sunrise, which was the important thing.

As I thought of that, I realized our stupidity: we hadn't checked to make sure there was a passenger train running at night.

Looking at Dahlia with wide, panicked eyes, I hissed my worries in her ear. "What if there isn't a train coming?"

She waved off my concern, heading toward the ticket booth. "Don't be ridiculous. The Klatch isn't stupid. This is the only way out of the area for us without some serious hoofing it, and that's not very practical when you burn up in the sun, you know? So they made some arrangements with the rail station to make sure that they always came through here in the night or the wee hours of the morning."

Something eased in my chest. "How do you know that?" I asked, remembering my earlier worry that everyone had the same trial.

She lifted her shoulders. "My dad is Vincent Ambrose. I know everything." She sent me a wink then giggled. I couldn't tell if she was kidding or not.

We got our tickets—Dahlia had that covered, too, since my inheritance was mainly in the form of golden coins that weren't really in human circulation—then headed to the train. We had packed light enough that we could keep our things with us instead of throwing them on the luggage cart, which I was grateful for. I had all my important things in my shoulder bag, but I didn't want to get stuck without clean underwear.

I followed Dahlia down the passenger car toward a couple of empty seats. I was grateful to see that there weren't that many people aboard, mostly because I knew instantly that they were human. I'd never seen a human in person before, and I was both startled and sort of disappointed to see that they basically looked like us.

Well, us with a tan and brown eyes.

Dahlia picked a seat toward the back of the car and settled in. I slid in beside her, letting out a sigh at finally being able to relax. That walk had taken a lot out of me, and even though I recovered quickly, I was still dead tired.

I was drifting off to sleep when Dahlia suddenly shook me. "Bronwyn!" she hissed in my ear.

My eyes forced themselves reluctantly open again. "What, Dahlia?" I asked impatiently.

She pushed in close to me, then pointed across the car toward a group in front of me. I was about to ask her what her problem was when I noticed who they were. Dark, sleek hair. Pale skin. Bright blue eyes. They were vampires, but not just any vampires.

"Oh my Hades. Those are the Petrovics."

Simultaneously, we ducked down in our seats, instinctively trying to hide. I told myself it didn't matter, that Ambrose Petrovic knew what my trial was and surely understood that this was the only way to find humans, but instinct is a powerful thing to try and ignore. On top of that, I wasn't sure that having Dahlia spotted with me was a good idea. And what if they found the message Corrine left me?

"We need to get out of here before they see us!" I hissed to Dahlia.

She nodded. We scooted out of our booth and darted out of the car, disappearing into the one just past it which happened to be the luggage cart.

"Do you think they saw us?" Dahlia asked just as the door opened again behind us.

Standing in the doorway was none other than Alexandre Petrovic. "What in Hades do you two think you're doing here?" He looked seriously angry, and I thought it might be due to worry over Dahlia—except he kept staring at me.

"Uh..."

I glanced over at Dahlia in search of help, but she just shook her head and shrugged her shoulders.

When neither of us answered, Alex made a frustrated sound. He ran his hands through his thick dark hair. "I thought I told you to be *careful*, not draw as much attention to yourself as possible!"

Dahlia glanced between us curiously, but if she was even the slightest bit jealous, it didn't show.

"Do you understand that my father and both my brothers are in the other room? And that if they see you there will be some serious questions?"

Alexandre had two older brothers, Desmond and Cather, who were much like their father. Cold and unapproachable, not to mention uptight and superior. Not exactly the kind of people I wanted anything to do with. Thankfully, they felt the same about me and were old enough now that I didn't ever have to interact with them.

Except, apparently, on a train to Transylvania.

I straightened my shoulders and tried to bluff my way through this. "Did it ever occur to you that I'm on this train to complete my trial?" I folded my arms across my chest, doing my best to appear like I was completely in the right.

I must have failed. "With Dahlia?"

I glanced at the other girl, then winced.

"What are you really doing, Bronwyn?" he asked in a quiet voice that was almost... tender?

Lying to him again and sticking to my story was probably the best option, but something made me want to trust Alex. He'd warned me. He said he wanted to be my friend. I decided to take a risk before I'd had time to think about it. "I need to find a Harker."

He stared at me.

Sighing, I reached into my bag and pulled out Corrine's note. I went over the whole thing with him, minus only my trial and my theory that either everyone was told to drain a human—which was seriously not sitting well with me—or that at least Corrine had been given the task too. And failed.

The train lurched and we all slipped sideways before righting ourselves again.

"Look, this is all crazy. I don't know what that note means, but I suggest you get off at the next stop and turn back around. Head back to the school and forget all of this."

That wasn't going to happen and he must have seen that in my face because he sighed.

"It's not just my family on this train. The Klatch is here too. If they, like me, don't believe that you're here for your trial, then you'll be made to speak the truth—about the note and whatever you know about this Harker." He paused, then added, "They won't like the connection to the Van Helsings."

No, and honestly, I didn't either. The idea that their family used to hunt my kind wasn't filling me with warm and fuzzies, but I didn't have a choice. I had to do this.

"Then it would be really good if they didn't see us, right?"

Alex's mouth pursed together; he didn't like what I was saying.

"We can't get off until the train stops anyway. Might as well see this through."

He didn't look happy, but nodded. "Fine. Do what you need to, but be careful. Don't let the Klatch see you—and if you find this Harker guy, *don't* tell him what you are. They may be scholars now, like the books say, but they once were responsible for the deaths of thousands of our kind. That sort of legacy isn't forgotten easily."

He told us to remain with the luggage at least until our stop, which was the second stop. After that, we wouldn't have much time before sunrise, and we'd have to work hard to avoid the Klatch. As it turned out, they were heading to Transylvania too.

"Wait there on the platform in the little shop there. I'll meet you there."

With a lingering look in my direction and barely a glance at Dahlia, he turned and left, presumably to rejoin his family.

"Well. That was weird," Dahlia commented.

I nodded. "Yeah. It was."

❧

The train arrived about an hour before sunrise, maybe less. We snuck off the train, keeping an eye out for the Klatch. Once we were on the platform, I was headed to the little shop where Alex had told us to meet him, but Dahlia stopped me.

"Wait. Are we seriously going to trust him?"

I stared at her in surprise. "Why wouldn't we?"

She rolled her eyes. "Because he's a Petrovic!"

"So? You're an Ambrose."

She lifted her chin a little, looking down her slender nose at me. "That's different. Besides, I don't have my whole family here with me."

I bit my lip. Why didn't she want to trust Alex? I didn't have an answer, but I knew that I still wanted to trust him.

"Look, we don't have time to wait around for him. Who knows how long it'll take him to get away from his family. And we don't have long before daylight. What if we get stuck here?"

In the end, it didn't matter if I wanted to wait for Alex or not. She was right. We didn't have time to wait around. "Let's at least ask if the people in there know where we can find the Harkers."

She reluctantly agreed. We went inside the little gift shop. There was only one old woman behind the counter, flipping through a magazine listlessly. When we asked her about the Harkers, she said that there was a shop just down the street that was a Harker Bookstore. It was the only Harker she knew. We thanked her and left before Alex made it to the gift shop.

Chapter Eight

Thankfully, the shop really was just down the street because the sky was already starting to lighten with the approach with dawn. In only a few minutes more, dawn would break, and we'd have some serious issues to deal with.

Like where we'd wait out the day.

Without anywhere else to go, we hurried into the little shop, surprised that it was open so early in the morning. Humans generally kept daylight hours only. The little bell over the door chimed, and we walked into a bookstore. It was an interesting mixture of modern and vintage, with the unique smells of books and old leather permeating the air. There were dozens of bookcases creating a maze out of the large space, interspersed with tables and the occasional reading chair. At the front, near the door, was the front counter with and vintage cash register.

Standing behind the register was a young man, maybe a couple of years older than us, with dirty-blond hair that was just a little too long and basic brown eyes. He looked up when we entered and those brown eyes went wide.

"Jesus," he whispered.

Instantly, he went around the counter and stepped between us, grabbing either of our arms. "Come, quickly. Dawn is nearly here."

I stared at him in surprise. Clearly, he was human, yet he seemed to know what we were.

Dahlia jerked her arm from his grasp. "We're not going anywhere with you."

He rolled his eyes at her. "We don't have time for this. Either come with me, or burn. It's your choice."

And presented with that option, we let him lead us. We went up the stairs and into a small room that had a bed and a chair, but was otherwise mostly empty. There was a stack of books piled haphazardly in the corner though. And there were windows. Large windows.

Dahlia noticed them too. "What in Hades—we'll burn alive in here!"

But the man ignored her. He went to the windows and drew large, heavy drapes across the windows until the room was so black, I was certain he couldn't see. He struck a match and lit a candle, then he asked, "Where's Corrine?"

"What? How do you know Corrine? Are you the Harker?" I asked, one question following the other instantly.

He made a frustrated sound in his throat. "I'm Abraham Harker. I assume she sent you to me."

I opened my mouth to answer that she had sent me to him—in a way—but didn't get the chance. Suddenly, there were loud shouts coming from downstairs. Harker turned toward the door, frowning. "Stay here," he ordered, then he turned and headed out the door, pulling it closed behind us.

I shared a look with Dahlia.

"So he knew Corrine. That means he's the one we're looking for, right?" Dahlia asked.

I shrugged. "I don't know."

The shouting downstairs got louder, and when we heard a thundering crash, the two of us reacted the exact same way: we ignored Abraham Harker's order and left the room.

On the balcony upstairs that overlooked the floor below, I saw Alex and froze. *What is he doing here?* That's when I noticed the rest of his family was there too. And they were fighting. The store had been empty when we arrived, but there were a dozen people in it now, including Abraham, and about half of them were on the floor, not moving. The Petrovics were chopping the men and women down like they were nothing, sending them crashing into bookcases with such force that the wood broke.

But what had me frozen to my little spot on the floor was Alex. He was facing off against Abraham, looking more terrifying and vicious than I had ever seen him before. He went at Harker and the "No!" escaped my lips before I could stop it.

He froze immediately, his blue eyes jerking up to where I was standing. Something flashed across his face, something like guilt or shame or just pain, maybe. That moment was enough to give Abraham time to swing a metal fire poker at his head.

"Alex!"

It cut along his forehead, opening a gushing wound, and he went down. His body collapsed on the floor and he was unmoving.

"We have to help him!" I shouted, hurrying down the stairs.

"Bronwyn, wait!" Dahlia called after me. A second later, I heard her light footsteps following after me.

I was headed straight toward Alex, but Abraham caught me around the waist. "No! Go, get out of here before—"

Dimitri Petrovic, member of the Klatch and Alexandre's father, held open a book and set it on fire. He watched it burn for just a second, then the fire jumped. It jumped to everything in the room that could burn, catching all at once. In seconds, we were surrounded by a blaze that was on the very short list of things that could easily kill a vampire.

Behind me, Dahlia screamed.

I coughed, my eyes seeking out Alex who was still unconscious on the floor.

Abraham still had his arm around my waist and was jerking me back, away from Alex. "We have to go!"

But I struggled free. "We can't leave Alex!"

"He's a Petrovic!"

Under normal circumstances, I would have been shocked that Abraham, a human, would know who Alex was, but right now, all I was worried about was the boy unconscious on the floor. The other Petrovics, Alex's own family, were exiting the burning building quickly. They were leaving him to burn!

But I wouldn't.

I hurried to his side and knelt down next to him. "We can't leave him! Please!"

Dahlia made a frustrated sound, but then, suddenly, she was on Alex's other side. "Fine. Let's go."

Abraham cursed and seemed none too happy to bring Alex along, but the building was burning and I refused to go without him. Finally, Abraham relented. "Fine! Bring him."

Hoisting Alex up between the two of us, Dahlia and I followed Abraham through the burning building. He led us to a door that went down. It opened up to an underground tunnel. As the fire burned above, the wood grew weak and collapsed above us, blocking the entrance. We ran down the cool, damp tunnel, dragging Alex with us. If we'd been two human girls, I doubt we could have done it.

Up ahead, Abraham led the way. He turned left, then right, then left a dozen times until I couldn't keep up with it. Finally, the tunnel opened up and the four of us burst into a room.

"Where are we? What... what's going on?" I asked, feeling winded and breathless.

As I looked around the room, I saw something move. Or more like someone. A young woman my age stepped forward. Her features were... familiar. Dark-red hair spilled over either shoulder, silky and smooth. Freckles dotted her pale skin and her wide eyes were a vampire-blue. It was impossible, but she was a vampire. One that, somehow, I had never met.

"Welcome. I'm Brigid."

"My Hades, Bronwyn!" Dahlia gasped. "She looks just like you."

Before I could ask, Abraham rounded on me. "Where is Corrine?"

I glanced at Dahlia, then said, "She... she left me a note. To 'find the Harker.' I assume she meant you."

He frowned. "Why didn't she just bring you here herself?"

I blinked at him. "Because she was exiled. She can never return—" But I didn't get the chance to finish. Rage overtook his features.

"You mean she was *murdered*. By him." He pointed at Alex.

"What? No! Alex would never do that! Corrine is *exiled*! She's—she's alive! Somewhere." But suddenly, I wasn't so sure. I wasn't so sure of anything.

He laughed at me and it wasn't a happy one. "You don't know anything. Corrine was one of us." He gestured toward himself and Brigid, who was studying me closely. "Corrine was trying to stop the Klatch from eradicating those they felt were *tainted*, unworthy. Vampires with some human lineage in them."

My eyes went wide, but it was Dahlia who spoke. "All vampires are pure. None would ever mix with a human." Her voice was cold and there was no question that she didn't like Abraham— and maybe not any human at all.

Abraham ignored her, focusing on me. "Humans and vampires don't have to keep killing each other. That's why my family stopped associating with the Van Helsings. We had a falling out, a disagreement. We saw some good in them." His gaze lingered on Alex and it was in direct contradiction with his words. "And there were vampires who agreed with us, who wanted to be friendly with one another. Corrine was working with me in the hopes that we might convince those on either side to see things our way. The Klatch, the Van Helsings... we had to stop them both."

"The Van Helsings died out a long time ago," Dahlia pointed out snidely.

Abraham smirked at her. "Is that what you've been told?"

Dahlia's face turned to stone, a lick of fear flickering in her eyes.

Turning back to me, Abraham continued, "As it turns out, there are even benefits to mixing our kinds. Half-breeds like Brigid—" he motioned toward my look-alike beside him, "—can walk in daylight, a mix of both worlds if you will."

I reeled from that bit of information, but was still confused about Corrine's involvement. "I don't understand, though. How did Corrine get wrapped up in this?"

Abraham smiled softly. "Because she was only half vampire."

I stared. It was impossible. I'd known Corrine forever. She was my only friend. I would have *known*—

But she didn't look like the others. Shorter, heavier. Just not as... flawlessly, coldly beautiful like the other vamp girls. Could it be?

"But—"

Brigid stepped forward and I was shocked when even her voice sounded so much like mine. "There is only one way to become full vampire—to drain the blood of a human completely."

I stared at him as things began to fall into place.

Corrine failed her test.

Because it was the same as mine and she was unwilling to kill.

And the only reason that *I* would be given the *same* test was that I was also—

I stared at the girl who supposedly looked so much like me. "Who... who were your parents?"

She smiled at me, not unkindly. "I never met my father. He was a vampire and he's dead now. But my mother was a human and she did her best to save my life. She got me to the Harkers. Then she died."

I wanted to ask her more questions, but I was afraid. Afraid of what she might tell me. So I turned back to Harker. "I... I think... ."

"You're a half-breed too," he finished for me.

Dahlia took a step away from me. That might have hurt if I hadn't been reeling from the shock of it all. "It's not possible," I whispered, but I knew that wasn't true. My father had died before he could tell me who my mother was, before he even had the chance to raise me, and I'd never even known her.

She could have been human.

"Which is why you should fight with us."

That got my attention. Immediately, I started to shake my head. "No. This is all—no. You're wrong. Corrine's alive. I'm not a half-breed, because there are no half-breeds and—"

"The truth is right in front of you, but you believe what you want," he told me. "Just know your options and what they mean."

"Options?"

"You can either return to the Klatch and face certain death, or you can stay here and fight. There are no other options."

But which one would let me live longer?

www.ingramcontent.com/pod-product-compliance
Lightning Source LLC
LaVergne TN
LVHW040159080526
838202LV00042B/3231